**J MACINTOSH**
**Macintosh, Cameron,**
**Selfie search /**

SELFIE SEARCH

An imprint of Enslow Publishing

WEST **44** BOOKS™

CAMERON MACINTOSH
DAVE ATZE

**Please visit our website, www.west44books.com.
For a free color catalog of all our high-quality books,
call toll free 1-800-542-2595 or fax 1-877-542-2596.**

Cataloging-in-Publication Data
Names: Macintosh, Cameron. | Atze, Dave, illustrator.
Title: Selfie search / Cameron Macintosh, illustrated by Dave Atze.
Description: New York : West 44, 2020. | Series: Max Booth: future sleuth
Identifiers: ISBN 9781538384657 (pbk.) | ISBN 9781538384640 (library
bound) | ISBN 9781538384664 (ebook)
Subjects: LCSH: Detective and mystery stories. | Street children--Juvenile
fiction. | Cell phones--Juvenile fiction.
Classification: LCC PZ7.M335 Se 2020 | DDC [F]--dc23

Published in 2020 by
Enslow Publishing LLC
101 West 23rd Street, Suite #240
New York, NY 10011

Cover design and Illustrations: Dave Atze

Typesetting: Think Productions

Printed in the United States of America

CPSIA compliance information: Batch #CS19W44: For further information contact
Enslow Publishing LLC, New York, New York at 1-800-542-2595.

# MAX BOOTH
## FUTURE SLEUTH

SELFIE SEARCH

CAMERON MACINTOSH

DAVE ATZE

*For Julian*

# CONTENTS

# CHAPTER 1
# A Spark of Excitement

Has anyone ever told you how hard it is to sleep beside a dreaming beagle-bot? Probably not – most people don't realize that beagle-bots are meant to be left turned on at night. Their digital dreams help them process the day's events and store the day's memories – just like our dreams do. That's all well and good, but Oscar's night-time twitching and barking can keep me awake for hours.

This is one of those nights.

I've finally drifted into a semi-half, kind-of sleep at 8:05 a.m. when I hear a loud thud above my head. For a moment I think it's Oscar, leaping up to chase an imaginary cyber-cat. But then I hear a familiar voice.

"Max! Are you awake yet?"

"Well, I am now, Jessie ..."

"Sorry, pal. I kinda thought you'd like to see this one straight away."

"What's *this* one?"

"I was hoping *you* might be able to tell *me*!"

I sit up and switch Oscar to fully-awake mode. Then I step out of the packing case we use as our bedroom, and rub my bleary eyes.

My best pal, Jessie, is standing just behind our packing case. She's holding a black rectangular object in her hand and staring down at it with a puzzled look on her face.

It's part of Jessie's job to identify the objects that come to our home – the Bluggsville City Museum storeroom. When she needs help, Oscar and I are always happy to lend a hand, or a metal paw! These little jobs keep us alive. When Jessie identifies a new object, she gets paid a few extra dollars. When we identify an object for her, she gives some of those dollars to us. Oh yeah – she also lets us live in the storeroom for free! We'd probably be living on the street and foraging for food scraps if not for Jessie's friendship.

I'm yawning as loud as a mooing cow-borg when Jessie hands me the rectangular object. It's about 12 centimeters long and 6 centimeters wide. One of its sides is shiny, like glass. The other side seems to be coated in protective plastic.

It kind of looks like … nothing at all. It's probably the most boring object Jessie's ever brought to us – at least since the 1986 pencil eraser she'd mistaken for a chunk of 22nd century bubble gum.

"Hmm," I say, trying not to roll my eyes. "You woke me up for a shiny plastic brick?"

"It's definitely not construction material," she laughs. "Have a close look at the ends."

Jessie hands me the mysterious thing, and I look at it closely from top to bottom. There seems to be a press-able button at one end. At the other, I can see a metal-edged hole that looks like an in-built dock, and two little sets of holes that look like tiny speakers. Perhaps there's slightly more to this than I thought ...

"In my professional opinion," I say, "I think it's a pillow warmer from 2098."

"But look at that input dock," replies Jessie. "It looks a lot like the electrode dock from a hair-growth stimulator. They were huge in the 2050s."

"No way!" I yelp. "This is definitely some kind of sleep enhancement device. I might need to borrow it if Oscar keeps barking at night!"

We could argue about it all morning, but Oscar has different plans. His ears prick up and he stands on his hind legs like a startled hyper-hamster. Usually, this means he's seen a robo-rat across the storeroom, but not this time. No, this time, the robo-rat's right on top of our packing case!

Oscar leaps into my arms and tries to use me as a ladder to get to the top of the case. As he scurries up, I squeeze onto him. He squirms in my arms, but I hold on tight. These ridiculous rat chases usually end badly. Oscar breaks at least one body part, and I have to spend hours putting him back together again.

The robo-rat doesn't make things any easier. It leaps off the packing case and grabs hold of the nearest ceiling support beam. As it scuttles upward, I can feel Oscar's body heating up like a frying pan. He's squiggling like an overgrown cyber-slug.

"Oscar!" I yell. **"Control yourself!"**

Suddenly he stops still, but it's not because of anything I've said. There's a shower of sparks flying out of his back end! I have to drop him before he burns any more holes in my T-shirt.

**8**

As he slides down my leg, Oscar brushes against the mystery device, which is still in my right hand. A big **zap** of electricity bolts out of his tail and surges through the device. Oscar crunches into the concrete floor, but for a moment I forget all about him – all of a sudden, the shiny side of the device has started glowing! It definitely seems to be some kind of screen.

It starts off white, then turns a light blue. Then, it goes black again, and a time display flashes across it. As quickly as it appeared, the time vanishes and the display changes again. Now it's just a black background, filled with rows of colored symbols. At the bottom of the screen there's an icon of an old-fashioned phone receiver – the prehistoric kind, from when phones plugged into wall sockets! That kind of receiver hasn't been used for about 360 years, but I recognize it from the Telecommunications History display at the museum.

"This is incredible!" yells Jessie, her face lighting up like Oscar's sparks. "You've just reactivated a mobile phone from the 21st century – the 2030s or 2040s, I'd say."

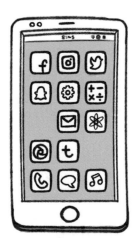

Jessie's a big fan of phones. She's uncovered lots of old ones that are now part of the museum's display.

I haven't been this happy since I rescued Oscar from the Lost Robo-dogs Home three years ago. But my smile only lasts a few seconds – the screen goes blank again, and stays that way. I shake the phone and push the button at the top, but the screen stays just as black and just as blank. As the phone fails to fire up, I feel my face going a very dark shade of red.

"Relax, Max," says Jessie. "It's probably just a flat battery. It's a miracle you got it working in the first place."

"A ten second miracle isn't good enough," I

moan. "I'm gonna get this thing working again if I have to swap half its parts with Oscar's."

Oscar whimpers and skulks toward the packing case.

"Just kidding, Oscar," I laugh. "Your parts are far too expensive to waste on an old telephone!"

"Anyway, I'll have to leave you to it," says Jessie. "I've got two hours to polish up an antique hover-scooter for the 22nd Century Fun and Fitness exhibition."

"Have fun, Jessie," I reply. "I'll hover-scoot into your workshop when I've got this hopeless thing working again!"

# CHAPTER 2
# Pedal Powering

I really should stop making so many big promises. I have absolutely no idea how I'm going to get this phone working again. All I can do is dig through Jessie's spare-parts boxes and see if anything useful might be lying around.

One thing I do know is – I'll definitely need some kind of cord that can fit into the input dock. That might give us some hope of connecting it to another source of power.

"Come on, Oscar," I yell. "Let's go hunting."

I tip two boxes over and we spread their

contents across the floor. Oscar sniffs at every broken gizmatron or ancient thingami-bot. After a few minutes, he looks up at me with a blank expression on his face.

"Hold on, Oscar," I say. "What about *this* old doo-gadget?"

I pick up a black plastic cord that looks like it might have broken off an old pair of headphones. One end is a sprawl of loose wire ends. At the other end, there's a connector that looks just about the right size to fit the phone's input dock. I try to slide it in, but it's slightly too wide.

"I've got an idea," I cry to Oscar. "Put that tail into spin mode!"

A second later, Oscar's rotating his tail so fast I

can barely see it. I slide on a pair of safety goggles and press the edges of the connector against his blurry tail. Sparks fly everywhere – at least this time they're not coming from Oscar's back end!

I move the cord away from his tail and look closely at the connector. We've definitely ground some of the metal off, but it's still too big to fit into the dock. I press it against Oscar's tail one more time.

After a second spray of sparks, the connector finally looks narrow enough to fit the phone. I push it into the dock and it slides in easily. It fits so snugly it doesn't wobble around, or fall out when I tip the phone upside down.

"That's a great start," I say to Oscar. "Now we just need to get some electricity going through it."

Oscar turns his tail off spin-mode and disappears behind a stack of boxes. Thirty seconds later, he's back, dragging an old tricycle between his metal jaws. He waves his paw at me and I follow him to an old treadmill in the far corner of the storeroom.

He drags the tricycle onto the treadmill, climbs onto it and starts pedaling. The tricycle stays in the same place as he spins the pedals.

"You're a smart animal, Oscar," I say with a wink. "But we need something to connect the wheels with the cord and the phone. Otherwise, your pedaling won't make any electricity."

Oscar nods slowly, as if to say, *Well, yeah, dummy!*

I snoop through another box of junk that Jessie hasn't yet found a home for. I find an old teddy bear from the 2070s, a broken toaster from the 1960s, and a make-your-own bubble gum machine from 2160. But it's something boring – an old bicycle light from the 1990s – that gives me a very big spark of an idea.

"These things made their light from pedal power," I tell Oscar. "Let's see if we can connect it to the tricycle … and then to the phone."

I shove the loose wire ends into a hole at the bottom of the light. Then, I clip it onto one wheel of the tricycle and ask Oscar to start pedaling. He spins his legs so fast I get dizzy watching them. And then … absolutely nothing happens.

"Faster, Oscar," I yell. "This absolutely has to work!"

Oscar pedals so hard his tongue hangs out and steam starts spewing from his joints … but it suddenly seems to be worth it. The phone flashes white, then blue, then black, and then we see the time display again.

At the top of the screen, there's now a little icon showing a battery. It's red, which probably means it won't last long if Oscar stops pedaling.

"It's okay, Oscar! Hop off and let me have a go."

Oscar flops onto the floor and I take his place on the tricycle. As I pedal, Oscar holo-projects an image of the battery graphic into the air above him. At first, it's only 4 percent charged. After five minutes of pedaling, it creeps up to 10 percent, but I'm already exhausted. I climb off and let Oscar take over, even though he doesn't look too happy about it.

We keep pedaling in five-minute shifts. After an hour of puffing and panting, we've got the phone charged to 82 percent.

"I think that'll probably be enough for now," I say to Oscar.

He smirks and thumps his tail on the ground. I think that's his way of telling me he agrees.

At least we've finally made some progress. I slide my finger across the phone's surface to see what it can still do. As I swipe from screen to screen, I see icons for maps, music, games and quiz questions. It's all pretty exciting until I press on the quiz and the map buttons, and nothing at all happens.

"Brilliant ..." I groan. "The screen works, but that seems to be about it."

I click on a few more icons and nearly jump out of my skin when one of them – a little icon of a camera – opens and fills the whole screen. The next thing I know, I'm looking at someone's digital photo album.

It feels a bit cheeky to open a stranger's photo album. But then again, the owner's probably been dead about 350 years. Hopefully they won't send an army of zombies to show their disapproval!

I tap on the first photo. It's a close-up of a young man's face. He'd probably be in his early twenties. He seems to have long hair, tied into a bun at the top of his head. He's smiling a goofy grin, and there's a pile of presents and balloons behind him.

I swipe across to the next picture and see the

same face, with an even bigger smile. This time he's wearing a bike helmet. He seems to be in the countryside somewhere, with real trees behind him. I open photo after photo and see the same face in different locations, laughing and smiling into his own camera.

"This is incredible, Oscar!" I yelp. "I really think Jessie needs to see this."

Oscar scurries off toward Jessie's workshop, and a minute later, the two of them appear beside the treadmill. Without saying a word, I hold up the phone to Jessie's eye level.

"Who's that?" she laughs. "And what's going on with his hair?"

"No idea, but he definitely liked looking at himself!"

"I wonder if we can find out more about him?" says Jessie.

Oscar seems to think we can. He bleeps loudly enough to get our attention. Then, he shoots a holo-projection of the photo into the air above his head.

Blown up ten times its original size, a little bit of text at the bottom of the photo becomes much easier to read. It's a time and a date on the photo:

**11:12 a.m., October 13, 2017**

"Wow," says Jessie, "2017! This phone's much older than I thought."

Oscar projects a collage of photos into the air, and Jessie and I step up and take a closer look at them.

I've never seen so many photos of the same face! If you ask me, it's kind of boring, but Jessie doesn't seem to think so. She lets out a loud gasp. "Holy cyber-snakes!" she yells. "Take a look at the one on the top right."

Oscar lowers the top-right photo to eye level

**25**

and I stare at it as hard as I can. I don't see anything too exciting about it – it's the same goofy face in some kind of public park. He seems to be holding a skateboard under his arm – an ancient one, with actual wheels on the bottom.

"Boring!" I groan. "Did this guy do anything but take photos of himself?"

"Look in the background, Max, behind his right shoulder."

I squint hard and see a metal statue in the background, a long way behind him. "Yeah? All I can see is a rusty old statue."

"That's not just any old statue," says Jessie. "Take a closer look."

I move right up to the projection, and Oscar

makes it even bigger for me. I can now see the statue in much more detail. It's a woman, cast in bronze. She's wearing long flowing robes, and a strange hat. She's also holding some kind of trophy in her left hand.

"Um, still slightly unexcited ..." I say to Jessie.

"That statue is none other than the glorious Nicole Squidman – a famous actor who won hundreds of awards. When she retired from acting, she went on to become Bluggsville's longest-serving mayor."

"What's that trophy she's holding?"

"It's an acting award she won in 2012. Back in the 21st century, they used to call these awards *Oscars*."

Oscar sits up on his hind legs and does a big bow.

"That statue you're looking at," says Jessie, "has been missing for about 250 years."

Suddenly I feel my heart pounding. "250 years?"

"And what's more, there's been a $7 million reward for it since 2244."

"Oscar," I say, looking down at his big electronic eyes, "is there any way you can tell us where he took that photo?"

Oscar shakes his head. It seems he's done all he can.

"Just a sec," says Jessie slowly. "Does the phone have a settings button?"

"Let's have a look."

I swipe back to the first screen and press every icon there is. The only other one that seems to work is a grey, wheel-shaped one. It takes us through to a list of phone functions. *Wallpaper, Notifications, Podcasts …* None of them mean a thing to me, until I scroll down and see a function named *Location Services.*

"I think you're onto something!" cries Jessie.

I hit the Location Services button and see another list of icons – miniature versions of the icons that were on the screen a few seconds ago. Each mini-icon has an on-off button beside it. The button beside the camera icon seems to be in "off" position, so I swipe it sideways and it changes color from grey to green. I don't know if I've achieved anything, but I flick back to the park photo and see if anything's changed.

Jessie suddenly gives me a big hug. "Look at the bottom of that photo!" she yells. "This is huge!"

I tap on the photo. It doubles in size, and I notice a small box on the bottom left side of it. It says:

**37° 48' 46.4" S, 144° 58' 11.3" E.**

"Unbelievable!" cries Jessie.

"Unbelievably boring!" I reply. "It just looks like math to me."

"**No, no, no!** Those figures tell us exactly where he was when he took the photo! If they're correct, the $7 million statue might still be in the same place."

Suddenly she's getting through to me. The mention of a $7 million reward seems to have blasted some of the wax out of my ears!

"How about we all go down now and see what's there?" I say.

"I'm stuck here today," replies Jessie, "but first thing tomorrow morning, we're there!"

Oscar wags his tail in approval.

"This could be a very big deal," says Jessie. "But don't tell anyone – if word gets out, there'll be 10,000 beagle-bots sniffing around with $10,000 bills in their eyes. And their owners, too!"

"Don't worry, Jessie," I say. "We've got 7 million very good reasons to keep our mouths shut!"

# CHAPTER 3

# Down to the Ground

That night, I'm lying in our packing case, snug as a slug in my warmest blanket, but I can't get to sleep. I can't stop thinking about that statue, and the $7 million that might go along with it ...

At 5:30 a.m., I give Oscar a nudge.

"Hey, Oscar," I whisper, "how about a little trip down to ground level?"

Oscar yawns and slowly stands up on all fours as I slip the phone into my pocket. He doesn't look too pleased, but he leads the way to the air-vent pipe we use to come and go when Jessie's not here. It's easy to enter from – it's just a quick slide down from a laneway up at street level – but it's not so easy to exit from. We have to climb on a packing case to reach the vent, then hoist ourselves up an old rope that Jessie attached to the top of it for us. It's hard work, but we're lucky to have it – Jessie would be in big trouble with the museum if they knew she was letting us live here.

We climb up and out, into the laneway at the top, and jog toward the Skyburb Down-station. When we get there, I look up at the schedule. Luckily, we only have to wait about ten minutes before our Skyburb – Skyburb 6 – pulls in above the ground-level docking station.

With the sun's first rays spreading across the land, Bluggsville looks like a beautiful canyon of tall buildings amongst the orange smog. As our Skyburb docks above the station and we step into our air cell, the sun hits my eyes. I have to close them and keep them shut as our cell hisses and shoots down toward the ground.

When we step out at ground level, there's hardly anyone around. Still, I make sure no one sees the ancient treasure I'm hiding in my pocket. I wait until we're in a dark alleyway before I take it out and turn it on. Straightaway, I bring up the statue photo and zoom all the way in to the location coordinates.

"Okay Oscar," I say, "remember these figures."

I read them out again, and Oscar shoots a holographic map into the air above his back. A white cross appears on the map in the exact location I've just given him. According to the map, the photo's location is about two kilometers from where we're standing at this very moment. It seems to be near one end of a large park on Bunjil Street.

It's a bit far to walk, so we run for the nearest zip-coaster station and leap over the barricades. A few seconds later, the next zip-coaster slides in. We climb into the first carriage and strap ourselves in. It takes off at high speed and zooms upward, looping-the-loop before we tip sideways, then upside down, then back to upright as we pull into the next station.

The park's only a short walk from the station. When we get there, we see a big green sign that says Griddle Park. Half of the park is a dusty paddock with a few wisps of grass peeping out of the ground here and there. The rest of the park is taken up by a hover-skate obstacle track. Even at this early hour – 6:33am – it's busy with hover-skaters, racing each other around and showing off their tricks.

"Can you show me the location for that photo again?" I ask Oscar.

Oscar brings the map up, and pinpoints the exact location. It's just beside the fence at the other end of the park.

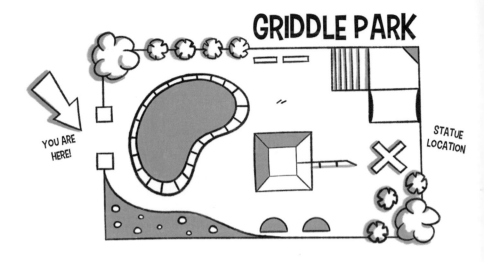

We run to the precise spot, but there's no sign of any statue. Then it occurs to me – this is where the photo guy was standing, not where the statue would have been. If I'm not mistaken, it would've stood right in the middle of the hover-skate track …

Oscar sighs and looks up at me.

"Yep," I agree, "it looks like the hover-skaters

have taken over the mayor's favorite hangout spot."

We run to the edge of the track. With all of those hover-skaters zipping past, it's way too dangerous to try to cross it. Our only option is to crawl across the dusty surface on our bellies.

"Alright, Oscar," I gulp. "Time to get our tummies dirty."

I lead the way, crawling on my stomach like a flat crab, and nearly choking on the dust.

It's just as well hover-skates really do hover. The skaters zoom over us with just a few centimeters of clear air above. As each skater flies over, their skates throw even more dust into our faces. This really isn't much fun, but we keep crawling for another ten meters.

"So," I yell to Oscar, "if I'm correct, we're just two meters from where the statue would have stood, all those years ago."

I ask him to activate his in-built metal detector.

At first, it only beeps when a hover-skate swishes over us. But as we crawl those last few meters, it squeals out a rapid pulse of beeps that get louder and louder as we wriggle forward. Finally, the beeps squawk like a police siren and Oscar's tail shoots straight up.

"It sounds like you've got something, pup!"

Oscar replies by popping out his claws and scratching at one particular spot on the ground. I crawl up beside him and try to dig with my bare fingers, but the ground is too hard for me to be much help.

After a few minutes of digging, there's a hole the size of a shoebox in front of Oscar. And then,

I hear myself gasping as the early morning sun catches hold of something shiny on the edge of the hole.

We throw our claws and fingers onto it, and very soon there's a metal head and torso, the size of my hand, sticking out of the ground. As we dig further, the ground starts to get a little softer. After a few more minutes of hard digging, we've revealed the entire body of a man, holding a long sword upright in front of him. He's only about two hands tall. The strangest thing about him is that he seems to have a life-size metal hand wrapped around his legs.

"Quick, Oscar," I say. "Take a photo of him and feed it into the Splinternet. We need to know who this could be."

Oscar does as I ask, but just before the Splinternet gives us a search result, we hear a loud whistle, and a voice booming through a loudspeaker.

"Skates off!" it yells. "Line up along the side of the track with your ID badges in your hands."

It's a very familiar voice – a voice that sends a very big shiver up my spine. "It's Selby," I whisper to Oscar. "I think we're in a bit of trouble ..."

My old friend Captain Selby ... Ever since we escaped the Skyburb 7 Home for Unclaimed Urchins two years ago, he's been trailing us up and down the Skyburbs of Bluggsville like a hungry hyper-hound. He has my picture on the back of the folder he carries around. So far, he's failed to catch us every time. But there's a first time for everything, and I've got a very bad feeling today could be it.

One thing I definitely know – we won't be joining Selby's ID line-up. We frantically shovel dirt back over the hand of our statue, and pat it down as hard as we can. Then, we crawl further across the track, scanning the ground for a dip or a ditch we can hide in. The best we can find is a little ditch in the dirt under a wooden jump ramp. We crawl in and curl up like sleeping sloths, but just a few seconds later, one of Selby's lieutenants lowers his head to our level and grabs hold of Oscar's tail.

It's all over.

"Let go of him!" I yell. "Take me if you have to, but leave my dog alone!"

The lieutenant doesn't take any notice of me, but Oscar nips his hand. He lets go of Oscar and grabs me instead, dragging me all the way out of the ditch. I've got no choice but to follow him over to the ID line-up, where the hover-skaters are already standing in a row. Oscar follows along, beeping like an angry parrot.

As soon as he sees me, Selby winks and cackles. "You're getting careless in your old age, Booth. Of all the places to find my favorite pair of rats … here?"

"Button your lips, Smellby," I hiss. "I'd rather be a part-time rat than a full-time parasite like you."

"There'll be plenty of parasites to play with where you're going back to," he laughs.

Selby's clearly found the one thing he was looking for. He lets the hover-skaters go back to their fun, and his squad makes a circle around Oscar and me.

I look down at Oscar, and he looks up at me. Both of our faces tell the same story – we're in big trouble this time. If they take me back to the home, they'll sell Oscar and wipe his memory. We'll never be friends again. And Jessie won't even know what's happened to us.

I've just about given up hope when I put my hand in my pocket and feel a familiar object in there. It's the phone, squished against my leg. I slide it up just far enough for a little bit of it to peep out above the top of my pocket, and then I cough at Oscar. He looks up and sees the phone, and gives me a wink.

The phone's still connected to the cord. I throw the end of it down to Oscar. Before any of Selby's crew knows what's happening, Oscar puts his tail into spin mode and brushes it against the wires at the end of the cord. A fresh charge of electricity pulses up the cord and into the phone – it even gives my hand a little zap.

I open the phone's camera and switch the flash unit on, and then – without any warning – I scream into Oscar's left ear. It gives him such a fright, he sends an extra jolt of electricity through the cord.

As the fresh charge hits the phone, the camera's flash unit lights up like a firecracker.

The lieutenant in front of me freezes. His eyes are so wide, he looks like a hairy tree frog! I look around and see the rest of the squad, squinting and blinking and trying to work out where they are.

Now's our chance. I leap onto the ground and crawl through the nearest pair of legs. Oscar follows close behind. While Selby and his friends shake their heads and stagger around in circles, we start running across the park. A few seconds later, I hear that familiar voice again.

"Nice move, Booth," yells Selby, "but not nearly as nice as this one."

I look back over my shoulder and see a huge net flying toward us. It's spreading out from the barrel of Selby's web gun. Before we know it, Oscar and I are both enclosed in a big black string net. It feels like we've been caught in a spider web. It feels a lot like we're about to be gobbled up, too.

All we can do is roll across the ground. As we roll, we drag the net onto the hover-skate track. It's a dangerous move, but it pays off. A second later, the nearest hover-skater zooms over the top of us. The white-hot hover-blades on the bottom of his skates slice through the netting, and make a hole just big enough for us to fit through. Just as Selby and his team reach the track, Oscar and I climb out of the net. We drop down onto our bellies and crawl across the track like a pair of hyper-charged jelly babies!

As we reach the far edge of the track, I look back and see the entire Recapture Squad on the track, doing their best to dodge the skaters. One of them isn't fast enough – a skater crunches into him and they both tumble across the ground. Selby manages to make it to the other end of the track, but by then we're already at the far end of the park, running as fast as we can.

As our feet thud onto the Bunjil Street footpath, Oscar uses his 3D printer to give Selby a little present. It's a brown plastic dog poo, with very slippery sides. He doesn't seem happy to leave just one – as we sprint away, he sprays the footpath with a smattering of plastic presents! They look incredibly real – the only thing missing is the smell.

The next thing we know, Selby's tumbling over the top of them and crashing onto the ground. Behind him, the rest of his team are still trying to make their way across the track, and getting angrier and angrier with the hover-skaters.

We don't stop running until we're safely back at the Skyburb Up-station. I finally dare to take another look over my shoulder. There's no sign of Selby. Even better, the signs tell us Skyburb 6 is only two minutes away from docking and sucking us straight back up to the safety of our storeroom.

# CHAPTER 4
## Another Excursion

Twenty minutes later, we're back at the storeroom. Jessie isn't there, and her workshop's locked up, but there's a note on our packing case:

**Gone to a meeting but noticed you weren't here. Tried to call you. Let me know you're ok.**

**J.**

"Oscar," I say, "did you have any missed calls while we were out?"

Oscar activates his display panel and we see two missed-call alerts, both from Jessie.

## Gulp ...

"What do we say to her?" I ask.

Oscar looks at me with a straight face and unblinking eyes.

"I know, I know ... the truth, the truth, but ..."

Oscar raises a paw into the air.

"Alright, Oscar. The truth! She may not like it, though."

I ask Oscar to send Jessie a text message, telling her we got a bit overexcited and went on a statue hunt ... and that we think we've found Mayor Squidman ... but that someone else might have seen her too.

Straightaway, Oscar's "incoming call" button

starts flashing. He opens his back panel and a small metal arm lifts out his phone goggles. I put them on and see Jessie's face, looking strangely pale.

"Max!" she yelps. "What happened?"

"Well, we checked out the coordinates, and yep,

there's some kind of statue there. It seems to have been buried for a long time."

"That's fantastic!"

"Well, yeah, except, we were digging it up when we were rudely interrupted by the Recapture Squad ..."

"Did they see what you were doing?"

"It's certainly possible."

Jessie looks down and sighs.

"I'm sorry, Jessie. Don't be angry."

"I'm not angry. I'd just hate Selby to be the one to dig it up. Who knows what he'd do with it. And he definitely doesn't deserve $7 million for *our* hard work."

"Don't worry," I reply. "We won't let that happen,

will we, Oscar?"

Oscar nods, slightly. I'm not sure he believes me.

"I can't even help you," Jessie says. "I'm in Zaggtown until tomorrow, on museum business."

"So, what should we do?"

"Nothing, until I get back. It's way too dangerous with Selby poking around."

"But Jess …"

"Promise me you'll keep out of his way. It's not worth going back to the Home for this."

"Okay … I, um … promise."

"Good to hear it. I'll see you tomorrow, okay? We'll sort it out."

By now, I'm so tired from all the morning's action, my eyelids feel like heavy curtains. Oscar's pretty worn out too. He's dribbling oil from the side of his mouth. He flops down onto his mat and I plug him into his charger. He powers himself down and comes to a complete stop in a pool of his own oil.

It's particularly cold in here today. I huddle in my blanket and push myself up against the walls of our packing case. As tired as I am, I'm still wide awake an hour later. All I can think of is that statue, and the bronze hand wrapped around it. Who knows if Selby and his team saw what we were doing. If they did, I could never live with myself if they dug it up and took all the credit for it – and all the money ...

Eventually, I drift off to sleep. When I wake, it's

8:45 at night! I throw the blanket off and tap on Oscar's power button.

"Sorry to interrupt your snooze, pup," I say. "How about joining me for another little excursion?"

Oscar yawns and points at the battery-charge monitor on his left front leg. It tells me he's only 40 percent charged. But, I figure that should just be enough to keep him awake for another visit to the hover-skate park. I change into some clean-ish clothes and carry Oscar back to the air vent.

Oscar clutches onto my back as I hoist us up to ground level. He takes another snooze as I carry him all the way to the Skyburb Down-station.

We have to wait 14 minutes before our

ZZZZZ<sub>z</sub>

62

Skyburb pulls in over the docking station. By now, it's 9:15 p.m. and the Down-station's completely deserted. We climb into the first available air cell and zoom down toward the ground.

Even at this hour, the city's still a whirlwind of light and color. Billboards and zip-coasters light up the city like daylight. As our air cell hisses to a stop at ground level, we tumble out and jump over the exit barricades.

When we reach the street, Oscar runs ahead of me. He's still got the destination coordinates saved into his memory banks. He completely forgets about the zip-coaster and runs ahead, but it's okay – I need the exercise!

Ten minutes later, we're back at Griddle Park.

I was expecting it to be dark and deserted, but there's a patch of soft light in the middle of the track. Something doesn't feel right. There are definitely no hover-skaters to get in the way, but it's clear that we're not alone.

My stomach turns to a bucket of acid as I look across the track and see five grown men hacking at the track surface with shovels – precisely where we uncovered Mayor Squidman's hand. One of the men is holding a thick torch and shining it down on the statue. We don't have to get much closer before we recognize the face of the man holding it – our dear friend Captain Selby.

"This is a disaster," I whisper to Oscar. "We've gotta stop them, somehow! Any ideas?"

# CHAPTER 5
# Night-time Fright-time!

We take shelter behind a bubble-bus stop on the other side of the street. From there, we watch Selby's team working, through a crack in the bus stop's concrete wall. We're still close enough to hear every word Selby says.

"Come on, sluggoes!" he grunts. "We need to get this thing uncovered before midnight. The truck's coming at 12:30. Then, we collect our paycheck and go out for a very expensive midnight feast!"

"Did you hear that, Oscar?" I whisper.

Oscar scratches his head as I take another

look through the crack. I can now see Mayor Squidman's hat-covered head, poking up in the middle of the track. I must say, there's something slightly familiar about her face. And then I realize, she reminds me of someone ... It's just enough to give me the tiniest spark of a plan.

"Hey, Oscar," I say, in my lowest voice. "Do you think it'll bother Jessie if we wake her at this time of night?"

A small smile appears around Oscar's mouth, and he winks at me. I think that's his way of saying Jessie won't really appreciate it. But we need her help, no matter how grumpy she's going to be!

"Alright Oscar, let's risk it! Get her on the line."

The panel on Oscar's back slides open again, and the metal arm lifts out the phone goggles. I grab them and slip them over my head.

I wait as the phone starts ringing through. It takes a very long time before a groggy voice says, "H-hello?"

"Um, hi, Jessie," I whisper. "It's us! I hope we didn't wake you."

Even Oscar seems to think that's funny. He smirks and rolls his eyes.

"Well, actually," says Jessie, "I was having a lovely dream about discovering a 1998 compact disc player, but I'll forgive you if you're calling with good news."

"Um," I say, "I'm not sure it's good news just

yet … but you might be able to help us with that."

"This sounds a bit worrying," she says. "Where are you?"

"We're down on the ground, looking at a certain statue you might be keen to see again."

I hear Jessie gasp. "Max, you promised me …"

"I know, I know, but I had a hunch someone might try to take credit for our discovery. It turns out I was right."

"Selby, huh?"

"You guessed it … but with your help, maybe we can stop him."

"Okay," Jessie sighs, "what incredible idea have you got for me this time?"

"Remember how you told me you did a bit of

acting in high school?"

"Mm-hmm …"

"How would you like to restart your acting career, like, right now?"

"Not really," she says, "but go on …"

"Well, I think you could do a really good impersonation of Mayor Squidman, with the right costume. Just a minute or two of your best acting, and I think we'll be fine."

There's a long pause before Jessie replies. "Okay, Max, if that's what it takes. Just don't ask me to sing!"

"Don't worry. I wouldn't wish that on my worst enemy – not even Selby!"

She laughs, but now isn't the time for jokes. I

take another look through the crack and manage

to get a better view of Mayor Squidman's outfit. It

looks like a thick, heavy robe.

"Hey Jessie," I whisper, "any chance you've got a

spare mayor's robe over there?"

"A spare *what*?"

"You know, one of those long black robey things

that mayors used to wear."

"Um, I don't have one of those at the moment," she says, "but let me see what I can dig out of my suitcase."

Jessie puts her goggles into camera mode so we can see what she's looking at. She seems to be staying in quite a nice hotel room. A few seconds later, we're looking directly into her suitcase.

Most of Jessie's clothes are jeans and T-shirts. There's nothing there that looks like anything Mayor Squidman might have worn.

"Sorry," she says, "this doesn't look very promising."

"Um, can I ask a strange question?" I reply.

"Well, it wouldn't be the first time!"

"So, um, what are you wearing at the moment?"

"Well, you just woke me up, so I'm currently wearing pajamas and a dressing robe."

"That's perfect!" I say, a little too loudly. "Just tidy it up a bit and you'll be ready for the stage!"

"But what about a hat?"

Once again I press my eye against the wall of the bus shelter and look through the crack. From here I get a nice clear view of Mayor Squidman's hat. It looks a bit like a pirate's hat I saw on display at the museum a few months ago.

I stop to think. "Right," I whisper, "grab a pillowcase off your bed."

"A pillowcase?"

"Just trust me!"

Jessie gulps and grabs a pillow from the bed. She slides the case off it.

"Excellent," I say. "If you stuff it with a few T-shirts and balance it on your head, I think you might just pass for Mayor Squidman."

"Sometimes I think you're very clever, Max …" she laughs, "but I'm not sure if now is one of those times."

At that very moment, Jessie completely vanishes from my goggles.

"Jessie?" I hiss. "Can you hear me, Jessie?"

I hear a little whimper down beside my feet. It's Oscar, pointing at his battery read-out with one of his front paws. He's already down to 19 percent.

"No, Oscar," I plead, "don't go into power-saving mode yet! We need to keep Jessie on the line."

He whimpers again.

"I know you're getting low, but you only need to hold out for a few more minutes."

Oscar goes back into full-power mode. He whines and shivers, but suddenly the glasses start working again. The next thing I see is Jessie looking in the mirror with the stuffed pillowcase on her head. I glance over at the statue and compare the two. The resemblance is far from perfect, but it might just do.

"So, what do you want me to say?" asks Jessie.

"Something like, *Go straight out that gate, or face your fate!*"

"Gee, I kind of like that," she says, and then she starts practicing it, in the lowest, scariest voice she can make.

"Okay Oscar," I whisper, "fire up your hologram projector!"

Oscar looks worried, and I know why – his hologram projector is a real drain on his battery.

"Don't stress, pup, we shouldn't need it for long."

Suddenly, a green, glowing vision of Jessie appears in the air above Oscar's back. She looks so ghostly, I almost get the shudders myself!

"Okay Jessie, that's perfect – just give us a few minutes and we'll be ready for showtime!"

Jessie gives me the thumbs-up, and I ask Oscar to put himself into low-power mode. We creep across the road, and when we reach the park, we hide behind one of the jumps in the hover-skate track. Here, we're only about 10 meters from Selby and his squad. They're all digging furiously.

I look down at Oscar's back again. His display panel says he's already down to 9 percent battery life. We don't have a second to lose. I nudge him until he steps out into the darkness, just a few meters behind Selby's back, and then I give him a nod. He sends a beam of green light into the air, and suddenly Mayor Jessie appears in glowing 3D form.

For a second she doesn't say anything, but then I put my hand up in front of my goggles and give her another thumbs-up sign. She removes her goggles and goes into character, repeating her *face your fate* line, again and again.

Oscar turns his volume up as loud as it can go, and Jessie's voice booms across the park.

**Go straight out that gate, or face your fate!**

Suddenly, Selby and his team freeze like startled

snowmen. They turn toward Oscar and look up at the creepy figure hovering above him. Even in the dark, I can see the color draining from their faces.

"Who *is* that?" yelps Selby.

Even I didn't think Selby was that brainless. But one of his assistants says, "It's her, it's her!" and points down at the statue, which is now half-uncovered in the ground.

They all start shaking and clutching at each other, and the next thing I know, they're sprinting away from us.

It's not a second too soon. Suddenly, the ghostly image fades and vanishes. Oscar's legs fold beneath him and he flops to the ground. All of his panel lights fade to black, too.

I put my hand in my pocket and grab hold of the old phone. The cord is still plugged into it. I slip the far end of the cord into Oscar's input jack, and his face suddenly comes to life again.

The charge from the phone bumps his battery life up to 5 percent.

"Quick, Oscar, put me back through to Jessie!" I yell.

A second later, I'm looking at creepy Jessie again. The pillowcase is now flopping halfway across her face. It makes her look just a little bit less scary.

"Did it work?" she asks.

"Did it *work*? You were incredible! You deserve one of those Oscar statues too!"

"Well," she laughs, "it's good to know I've got options if things don't work out at the museum."

"Anyway," I say, "do you think you could get over here soon? We need to make sure no one gets their hands on this statue before the museum does."

"Zaggtown's an hour away by zip-coaster, but I'll be there as soon as I can," she replies.

# CHAPTER 6
# A Grave Situation

Oscar fades out to zero again and goes to sleep, but this time I'm not so worried. I sit there scraping mud off the mayor's statue until Jessie shows up, just over an hour later, with three other staff members. I recognize one of them – Professor Wong – the boss of the entire museum. She's shining a torch onto the statue and looking at it closely.

"Incredible work, Max," Jessie whispers in my ear. "The people of Bluggsville will thank you for this … one day."

I know it won't be tonight. If Professor Wong

finds out who I am, and where I live, Jessie will be in all sorts of trouble. For now, I'm just a passing stranger with a sleepy beagle-bot.

"This looks very promising," says Professor Wong. "But before we get too excited, I need to see some proof that this really *is* the missing statue. We've seen hundreds of forgeries of famous statues in the last few years."

Jessie and I look at each other. She almost chokes on her words as she responds to Professor Wong. "Well … I do have the old photo that led us here. It's definitely good evidence, but it's not exactly proof."

She's right – after all, we can't even name the person who took the photo.

"Well then," says Professor Wong. "For now, we'll make sure the statue's protected from any greedy vultures. But … until you can give me some absolute proof that this really is Mayor Squidman, there's not much more we can do with it."

"Don't worry, Professor," says Jessie. "We'll prove it's the real thing, one way or another."

"You'll need to work quickly. We can only keep the statue protected for two days at most. The hover-skaters aren't going to be happy about it!"

Professor Wong asks her assistants to build a barrier around the half-visible statue. She stays there to oversee the construction while Jessie and I walk back to the docking station. As we walk, we brainstorm ideas to prove the statue really *is* the statue. Neither of us can think of anything that will be good enough for Professor Wong.

When we arrive back at the storeroom, we sag into chairs in Jessie's workshop. By now, it's 2 o'clock in the morning. We're all exhausted.

"So, what do we do now?" I ask.

Jessie's face is blank. Mine probably is too, but now that Oscar's plugged into a charger, he looks a lot more alive than both of us. His brain seems to be working a lot better too. He switches his projector on and grabs the phone out of my pocket. Then, he plugs it into one of his input docks, and a gallery of the owner's photos flashes into the air above him.

"Good thinking, Oscar," says Jessie. "Let's take a closer look at his photos. Maybe we've missed something."

Oscar flashes up photo after photo, as big as he can make them before they go blurry. Those 21st century phones were hopeless – their photos go blurry if you make them any bigger than a robo-rat! What a shame they didn't invent giga-pixel cameras a few years sooner ...

Jessie and I check each photo for details. We're still shocked by how much this guy seemed to like his own face! There's one picture of him shoveling a hotdog into his mouth. In the next picture, he's cuddling a baby pig!

Oscar flashes up photo after photo until we both stop and stare at a picture of the same mystery man, blowing out candles on a birthday cake.

"Stop right there!" yells Jessie. "This could be the one!"

We count the candles. There are twenty-one of them. Then, we look at the time and date information at the bottom of the photo – it was taken at 7:59 p.m. on November 12, 2017.

"That's very useful information," I say, and I do

some math in my head. "It means he must have been born on the November 12, 1996."

We look even closer and notice some writing on the cake. It's hard to read, but we can just make out what it says:

## Happy 21st, Will

"This just keeps getting better!" yells Jessie.

"So," I say. "We know his name is Will – probably William – and we know when he was born. Let's do a scan through the birth records on the Splinternet and see what else we can learn about him."

I look down and see Oscar shaking his head at me, like I've just made a really dumb suggestion. He's right – our mysterious friend Will was born well before the old Internet melted down in the Great Solar Flare of 2037. There won't be any birth record online. Oscar checks the death records and finds nothing there either – perhaps he died before 2037, too. It's almost like he never existed, except for the digital remains of his life in the phone.

"Don't worry," says Jessie calmly. "There are still plenty of old paper records on file. We'll just have to visit the government office and spend a few hours going through them."

"If they let us," I say. "I don't have a Paper-Handling License. And it could take weeks – we don't even know his surname."

"I know," replies Jessie. "I don't have a license either, but maybe Professor Wong could come with me. What other options do we have?"

"How about a little trip down to the Bluggsville West Cemetery? We might be able to find a tombstone with his first name and birthdate on it."

Jessie groans. 'That'll take even longer than going through the paper records. Are you sure you want to do that?'

"I'm not sure at all, but it'll definitely be more fun than paper files."

"It's up to you," she says, "but you'll have to go down by yourself, I'm afraid. I've just got too much to do here tomorrow."

"That's alright," I wink. "Oscar will save me from any more ghosts. I think I've seen enough of them tonight already!"

At 7:15 a.m., after just a few hours of sleep, Oscar and I take an air cell down to ground level. We walk the full twenty minutes it takes to get to Bluggsville West Cemetery. A shiver runs up my spine as we pass through the old metal gates and into a concrete forest of towering tombstones. I know we're looking for a needle in a haystack, but at least the graves are arranged by century, and also by decade.

Our friend Will was born in 1996, and we know he lived until at least 2017, so we head straight for the 21st century section and have a look around.

The graves from the 21st century are the most interesting of all. Back then, everyone was crazy about photos and videos, and a lot of people included a little video clip on their tombstone, so everyone could get to know a little bit about their life.

We start at the west section and walk east, checking the graves on either side of us for the name William, or a birthdate of November 17. As we walk, photos light up on the tombstones, and little video screens play clips of birthday parties and weddings. Someone even has a clip of a custard pie fight!

We've just entered the 2030s section when Oscar suddenly stops dead in his tracks. He's a few meters ahead of me, staring at a bright red pyramid-shaped tombstone. His tail vibrates in excitement as he lifts his front paw off the ground and waves at me to catch up with him.

I run along, and turn to see a big red pyramid with a round photograph at the top. It's a man who looks about 50, with gray hair and a big smile. There's no bun at the top of his head, but he still looks an awful lot like our old friend Will.

I look down at the inscription and see the name William Arnold Jaxson. It says he was born on

November 17, 1996, and died on April 7, 2036. He didn't live to be an old man, but I'm so happy we've found him I grab Oscar's paws and do a little dance in front of the tombstone. The cemetery's gardener sees what we're doing and shakes his head at us, so I figure we'd better tone ourselves down. I stand still and ask Oscar to take a photo of Will's tombstone. He prints out a copy for me and I slide it into my pocket.

"Now," I say, "do a quick Splinternet search and see if you can find any Jaxsons still living in Bluggsville."

Oscar sets his search mode into action and projects the results into the air above him. There only seems to be one Jaxson left in the entire city.

Her name is Helen, and she lives in Konnichi Street, Bluggsville South-West. According to the map that appears beside her details, she only lives a few streets from where we are right now.

"Fantastic, Oscar!" I yell. "Let's go and meet this mysterious Helen."

We wave William goodbye, and make our way back to the gateway. As we go, a video screen pops out from William's tombstone. Grey-haired William smiles and waves into the camera. Then, he puts his thumb in his mouth and blows a raspberry at us.

It's a shame we never met. I think we could've been good friends!

# CHAPTER 7
## Helpful Helen ...

Konnichi Street is long, but incredibly narrow. On both sides, it's crammed with high-rise apartment blocks. Helen lives at 546/76. Her apartment block is built to look like a huge metal banana. It even leans over to one side and seems to be peeling at the top.

Judging by Helen's address, it looks like she lives on the 54th floor. When we reach the main doorway, we press on the buzzer for apartment 546 and wait for a response. It seems to take hours, but finally, a face appears on the little video screen beside her number button. It's the face of a very *old* looking woman.

"Can I help you?" she says.

"Well," I reply, "this might seem a bit strange, but we're wondering if the name William Arnold Jaxson means anything to you."

Helen's eyebrows pull together and she looks at me with a frown. "And just who might be wanting to know?"

"Well, my name's Max, and this is my robotic super-assistant, Oscar."

"And why are you so interested in William Arnold Jaxson?"

"So, you *do* know who he was?"

"This is *my* home and *I* will ask the questions, young man."

Gosh, I wasn't expecting Helen to be so aggressive!

"I ask you again – how do you know who he was?"

"Well, it's a long story, but we just visited his grave, and we seem to have come across his old telephone."

"A 400-year-old telephone? What absolute nonsense."

"Well, it just so happens that I'm carrying that telephone in my pocket at this very moment."

"I think I've heard enough."

"Did you hear that, Oscar? She's heard enough – she believes us!"

I hold my left hand down to Oscar-level, but he doesn't high-five it. I look back up at the video screen. It's gone blank.

"Ms Jaxson? Can you hear me?"

I'm giving her button another push when the glass doors at the front of the building suddenly slide open. A colossal security guard storms toward us.

"I'll ask you nicely, just once," he says. "Get off this property, worm features."

He's obviously never heard that no one calls Max Booth *worm features* and gets away with it!

"Hey, Oscar," I yell. "Over there – a fat, juicy robo-rat!"

Oscar looks around, his eyes darting in all directions.

"Just in there – under the reception desk!"

For a moment, I don't think Oscar believes me, but the temptation is too strong. He darts toward the doorway and between the guard's legs. The guard dives over the top of him, but he's much too slow. Oscar zips through the doorway and the automatic doors close behind him. It's lucky they're made of glass – at least I can see him as he darts left and right in the foyer, desperately trying to catch sight of the non-existent robo-rat.

At least one of us has made it into the building. The guard looks fairly determined to stop that number going any higher. He steps back toward the doorway and stands in front of it with his arms on his hips. There's no way I can get past him. Instead, I give him a friendly wave and walk around to the side of the building. I wait there a few minutes, gathering my thoughts.

Without Oscar, I'm extremely short on techno-tricks, but I do have a 400-year-old phone in my pocket. It sets my mind racing.

When we pressed Helen's buzzer, I noticed an *Emergency access* sign, just above the door. I'm sure there was a phone number below it. I peep around

the corner and read the number again:

**0005-4754-389875**

If I can use it to cause a little distraction at the

reception desk … I might just be able to get inside.

There's no time to waste – who knows what Oscar's doing in there!

I take the phone out of my pocket and wonder if, just maybe, I can use it to make an old-fashioned phone call. The problem is, it doesn't want to connect to the Bluggsville phone network. I'm not surprised – it *is* 400 years out-of-date, after all. Still, I've got a few bits and pieces in my pocket that might bring it into the 25th century ... if I can just find a way to make the cord work as some kind of antenna.

I plug the cord back into the phone and throw the other end up until it catches on one of the building's communications cables. Then, I pull on the phone until the cord stretches tight. The cable doesn't carry electricity, but suddenly, I hear a strange buzz, and feel a fuzzy vibration in my hand. I look down at the phone's display. There's now a little symbol at the top that wasn't there before – it looks like a small triangle, made up of five lines.

I tap the phone receiver button on the screen and a keypad appears. I type in the *Emergency access number* and press the phone to my ear. It doesn't make a sound.

I'm about to throw the phone on the ground and jump on it 500 times when I hear a voice. "Hello?"

I spin around – I could've sworn it came from behind me. But then I hear it again, and realize it's coming from the ancient device in my hand. I press it to my ear and hear a third "*Hello?*"

"Um, hello!" I say, and then I pause to do some very quick thinking. "Yes, um, hi! There's been a terrible emergency at 76 Konnichi Street."

"What kind of emergency?" asks the voice.

"Oh, a very severe one! The guard seems to have fallen asleep at the desk. I can't get into my apartment!"

"That's dreadful. We'll send someone over immediately."

Then, I bump the call button and accidentally hang up. I try to re-enter the number, but the next thing I know, I'm talking to Mildred from Wimble's Dried Shrimp Supplies. She's desperate to sell me a year's supply of powdered brine shrimp. When I finally manage to convince her that I don't like seafood, I hang up and look around the corner again. There's already a security hover-cart at the front of the building.

The guard runs out from reception and talks to

his visitor through the hover-cart window. They both look confused, and then they start yelling at each other.

It's my only chance – before the first guard turns around again, I run on tiptoes to the doorway and sprint at top pace into the reception area. At first, there's no sign of Oscar, but I need to get out of sight before any more company arrives. I run to the lift and hit the button for the 54th floor. The lift door doesn't want to open. I look up at the floor display panel and see that it's still up at floor 70 ...

I hit the button another five times, but the lift creeps down with painful slowness. By the time it's reached the 30th floor, I can see the guard walking back toward the doorway with a very unhappy look on his face. As he enters the building, I look up to the display again – still ten floors to go! All I can do is hide behind a big potted plant near the lift door and hope the guard doesn't look this way.

A few seconds later there's a *ding* as the lift door opens. I jump out from behind the potted plant and run toward it, as an angry voice yells, "Hey!"

I tumble into the lift and hit the "54" button. Just as the guard's face appears in the doorway, the doors slide shut and the lift shoots upward.

I take a deep breath, and feel a little bit better until I feel a bump on the back of my knee. I jump so high I nearly crunch into the roof. When

I land, I turn around and see Oscar looking up at me from the floor. He's grinning a *"that's what you get for lying about robo-rats"* grin, and wagging his tail.

"Oscar! I'm sorry, but hey – we're in, aren't we?!"

Oscar nods and nuzzles my knee as the lift slows down and halts at the 54th floor. The door opens and we follow the signs to the big blue door of number 546.

I take a deep breath and press the buzzer. Almost immediately, the door swings open and we find ourselves face-to-face with Helen.

"You!?" she cries. And then she starts yelling, "Security! Security!"

"No, please, just hear me out," I beg.

"You shadies think I'm a walking money tree," she howls. "Well, you won't be getting any of *my* ..."

"We don't want your money!" I yell. "And don't call me a shadie!"

There's nothing I hate more than being called a shadie. It's not my fault I can't afford to live on the ground, or buy nice clothes. And it's definitely not my fault the Skyburbs cast shadows over the rest of the city!

Before I say something I might regret, I take the phone out of my pocket and open it to the first photo of William I can find. At the same time, Oscar prints another photo of William's tombstone and lifts it up as high as he can.

Suddenly, Helen falls silent. Her eyes triple in size as she takes in the photos. Then, she stares at the phone, and a small tear drips down her cheek.

"I'm so sorry," she says. "William was my great, great, great, great, great, great-grandfather. But, why is he of so much interest to you?"

"Well, I think this phone might have belonged to him."

"Please, come inside."

We follow Helen into her apartment. It's very cozy – full of old paintings and furniture, and a collection of antique tennis rackets from the 2250s.

I tell her how Jessie came across the phone in the museum's storeroom. I also tell her about the statue, and how we urgently need to confirm it's the real thing.

"This is incredible," she says. "Nicole Squidman was William's favorite actress. He met her once, with a cauliflower in his hand. She signed it for him, but sadly, my great, great, great, great, great, great-grandmother got hungry and ate it."

"That's a tragedy," I say. "Can you tell us anything else about William's life?"

"Just a little," says Helen. "According to my great, great, great, great-grandmother, he spent so much time taking photos of himself, he never finished high school. But he did set up a successful photography business, helping people look better in photos from their own phones."

When Helen finishes her story, I tell her that her great, great, great, great, great, great-grandfather and his phone have done an incredible service to the people of Bluggsville. He's helped us rediscover a treasure that's been missing for hundreds of years.

Helen looks extremely proud. "Let me know if there's anything I can do to help you," she says. "I've always wanted to dig up buried treasure!"

# CHAPTER 8
## Shiny Squidman

The next Monday, I'm down at Griddle Park with Oscar, Jessie and a bunch of her coworkers from the museum. We're all here to celebrate the return of Mayor Squidman's statue to the people of Bluggsville.

Helen's here as the guest of honor. Professor Wong's here too, holding a pair of scissors to cut the ribbon in front of the statue.

There's now a viewing platform all the way around the statue. It was much too heavy to move, so they left it exactly where it was. According to

Jessie, the $7 million reward was just enough to build the platform ...

I'm a little disappointed that none of those dollars ended up in *our* pockets, but at least Selby didn't get his hands on them either!

Just before she cuts the ribbon, Professor Wong stops and hands the scissors to Helen. Helen looks a bit embarrassed, but she cuts the ribbon like a true professional. Then, she takes a phone out of her pocket and photographs herself smiling in front of the statue. She gives me a wink as everyone claps and cheers. Even the hover-skaters seem to enjoy the show – but maybe they're just glad to be getting their park back again!

Mayor Squidman is shining and smiling. It's hard to believe she's been standing in the same spot for nearly 400 years. She doesn't even look tired!

When the crowd finally breaks up, Jessie comes over to Oscar and me, and rubs us both on the head. "I'm really sorry you guys didn't get the credit for this," she says sadly. "I'll make sure you get it one day."

"That's okay," I reply. "And I'll make sure you never have to wear a pillowcase on your head again – unless you liked it!"

"That's a relief," she says. "There's only space for one Oscar in *my* storeroom!"

## --- THE END ---

## Sleuth Truth: Mobile Phones

Until the late 1990s, most people made their calls using phones that plugged into the wall and stayed in one place. By the year 2000, however, more and more people were carrying much smaller phones wherever they went.

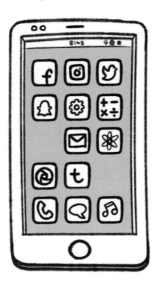

The first mobile phone, made in 1973, weighed more than 2 pounds! Mobile phones became available to the public in 1983, but few people could afford them. By the mid-1990s, they had become much cheaper, and easier to carry around! Before long, they had excellent cameras, and were able to connect to the Internet. Today, most phones are more like small computers that can make phone calls!

## How they work:

When you make a call on a mobile phone, the phone changes the sound of your voice into an electronic signal, and sends it out as radio waves. When someone answers your call, their phone receives the waves and changes them back into the sound of your voice.